8/21   4/22

BJ

D0951916

IS THE
HERO
OF
EVERYTHING

LOOK FOR IGGY'S OTHER TRIUMPHS

The Best of Iggy

Iggy Is Better Than Ever

IGGY

IS THE
HERO
OF
EVERYTHING

WITHDRAWN

ANNIE BARROWS

ILLUSTRATED BY SAM RICKS

putnam

G. P. Putnam's Sons

G. P. Putnam's Sons
An imprint of Penguin Random House LLC, New York

Text copyright © 2021 by Annie Barrows
Illustrations copyright © 2021 by Sam Ricks

G. P. Putnam's Sons is a registered trademark of Penguin Random House LLC.

Visit us online at penguinrandomhouse.com

Library of Congress Cataloging-in-Publication Data is available.

Printed in the United States of America
ISBN 9781984813367

1 3 5 7 9 10 8 6 4 2

Design by Marikka Tamura
Text set in New Century Schoolbook LT Std.

CONTENTS

CHAPTER 1

FOOD FOR THOUGHT

There are plenty of people in this world who eat squid. Nobody's *making* them eat it. They like it. "Squid cooked in squid ink!" they say. "Can I have seconds?"

There are some people who think cheese is a dessert. They go to a restaurant, and instead of cake or pie or an ice cream sundae, they say "Oh, I'll have the cheese! Yum!"

What do we learn from this?

That some people are bonkers?

No!

We learn that different people have different opinions. They have different points of view. From *my* point of view, eating cheese when you could have cake is weird. But from the point of view of the cheese eater, that is one tasty hunk of cheese!

Here's another way to say it: The cheese eater and I have different interpretations of the word *dessert*.

And guess what! Neither of us is wrong. I can say to the cheese eater "Eat your cheese in peace and happiness, you cheese eater! More cake for me." And the cheese eater can say—

Wait. No, he can't. His mouth is full. Gross!

Are you wondering if this whole book is going to be about cheese?

It isn't. I think I'm done talking about cheese.

The important thing is this: People can have different points of view about a thing (like dessert) or about an event (like a kid jumping off a roof). Two people can look at a kid jumping off a roof, and one will say "That's bad!" and one will say "Wow! Cool!" and it is possible that both of them are right. They have different interpretations of the same event.

Obviously, there are some things that can't have different interpretations. Like a cat. A creature either is a cat or it isn't a cat. You can't look at a crocodile and say "In my opinion, that's a cat."

Well, you can. But you'd be annoying and also possibly eaten.

Facts stay the same, while words and ideas and events are open to interpretation. Got that?

You sure?

IGGY

Good, because several of the things Iggy Frangi does in this book are, apparently, *open to interpretation*. Some of you may have already met Iggy,* but if you haven't, I'll tell you a few *facts* about him: Iggy is nine. He's in fourth grade. He's the main character of this book, which means he does most of the important things in it. There are people, like for example Iggy's mom and dad, and Rudy Heckie and Rudy Heckie's mom and dad, and Iggy's sister Maribel, who think that the things Iggy does are bad, even very bad. And irresponsible and careless and unsafe and— you know, *bad*. But some people, like for example Iggy and me, think that Iggy is brave and resourceful and caring and generous. In fact, we think Iggy is a hero!

THE FRANGIS

---

*Hi there! Good to see you again!

Clearly, people have different opinions about Iggy and the things he does. That is their right. Iggy and I will not stand in their way. We would simply like to point out

RUDY

that if Iggy does one or two or three things and then other people hurt themselves, that does not mean Iggy *caused* their problems. In our opinion, they caused their own problems. But we're not going to argue about it. No, we're not. We are willing to say to Iggy's mom and dad and Rudy Heckie and Rudy Heckie's mom and dad and Iggy's sister Maribel "Have your opinion in peace and happiness, even if you are completely wrong!"

MARIBEL

THE HECKIES

We are also willing to say that *you* can decide for yourself about Iggy, after you read about what he does. You are free to interpret Iggy's actions any old way you want: right or wrong.

But one thing is *not* open to interpretation, and that is how it began. It began with a fact, and the fact is this: Two days after Halloween, the Heckies' house was robbed.

CHAPTER 2

CANDY
IN PERIL

The Heckies were Iggy's neighbors. Their house
was only three houses away from Iggy's house.
If the thieves had been a little more energetic
and walked just a little farther, they might have
robbed Iggy's house. They might have sneaked
down the path beside Iggy's house, opened the
gate, gone into the back yard, stood on a garden
chair, smashed a window, climbed through it,
and stolen Iggy's parents' computers and Iggy's

9

mom's earrings and a jar with coins in it. They might even have poured orange juice inside their toaster, which, strangely, is something the robbers did in the Heckies' house. They did all those things in the Heckies' house.

Mr. and Mrs. Heckie came over to tell Iggy's parents about it. Iggy just happened to be in the kitchen at the time. He was looking at his Halloween candy. Only looking, not eating.

On Halloween, Iggy was allowed to stuff himself with candy, but after that, he could only have one piece after lunch and one piece after dinner, *if* he ate his vegetable. (And, boy, you want to know what's open to interpretation? The word *ate*.) When Mr. and Mrs. Heckie came over, Iggy had already yammed down his lunch piece of candy, and now he was laying his candy out on the counter to plan which one he was going to eat after dinner.

Fun size is not as much fun as regular size.

"I'm so sorry, Jan," said Iggy's mom in the next room. She had said this several times before.

"I feel like it's not even my *house* anymore," Mrs. Heckie said. She had said this several times before too. "Danita hasn't slept a wink since then." Danita was her daughter. She was thirteen and went to the same middle school as Iggy's sister Maribel. "And neither has Rudy."

Good, thought Iggy. Rudy Heckie was only seven years old, but for some reason, he thought he was the coolest kid in the world. He thought he was cooler than Iggy. Which he wasn't.

Then Mrs. Heckie said something shocking. "Can you believe they took all his Halloween candy? A little boy's candy? Why would they do something like that?"

Duh. Iggy knew exactly why they would do something like that. Candy is good. Everyone wants it, thieves included. Iggy looked down at the counter. He had a lot of good stuff left. Kit Kats. Two packs of Skittles. Reese's, not pieces, but whole cups, three packs of them. Eight candy bars of different kinds, all fun size, but still. One regular-size Twix. Four peppermint patties, which he liked and Maribel didn't, so he had traded two things of SweeTarts for her two peppermint patties. Plus, he had a bunch of less-good stuff, like lollipops and bubble gum and Laffy Taffy and those weird round hard candies that don't even have a name and hurt the top of your mouth.

Sitting there, looking at his candy, Iggy experienced two different kinds of fear, one after the other. The first fear was that his mom was about to say something like "I'm sure Iggy would be glad to share his Halloween candy with dear, sweet little Rudy."

Iggy quickly swept his candy into his bag, preparing to run away and hide with it.

But all his mom said was "I'm so sorry." Again.

What a great mom.

"We thought we should let everyone know," said Mr. Heckie in a deep, growly voice. "This could be the beginning of a crime wave, and we all need to be ready to defend ourselves."

"Thanks," said Iggy's dad in a not-very-growly voice.

A crime wave? Iggy experienced a second fear: What if thieves broke in to his house and stole *his* candy? He waited all year for Halloween candy.

Then Iggy experienced another fear, which wasn't really a third fear but an add-on to the second fear. What if thieves broke in to his house and stole not only his candy but the computers too? That's what they'd done at the Heckies'.

Then he would have no candy and no video games.

That would be bad.

"You folks have an alarm?" Mr. Heckie growled.

"Uh. No," said Iggy's dad.

"Might be time to get one," said Mr. Heckie.

"Thanks, Carl," said Iggy's dad again. "We'll give it some thought."

Some thought? They were in the middle of a crime wave! Iggy opened his bag and looked at his candy again. This was no time to think! This was time to protect his candy!

The following moment, Iggy got an idea.

Some people say it wasn't a very good idea, but they are wrong. It had three parts, this idea, so it was going to take some time. Some effort. Some sweat. But it was an idea that would save his candy, defend his family, and bring the crime wave to a crashing halt. It was, in other words, a brilliant idea.

Iggy zipped upstairs. There, part one began.

14

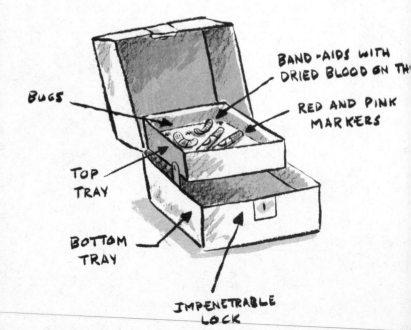

BAND-AIDS WITH DRIED BLOOD ON TH[

BUGS

RED AND PINK MARKERS

TOP TRAY

BOTTOM TRAY

IMPENETRABLE LOCK

CHAPTER 3

THE STRONG BOX

"Why did part one begin upstairs?" you ask.

Because that's where Iggy's strongbox was.

"Strongbox?" you ask. "What's a strongbox?"

You sure ask a lot of questions.

A strongbox is a strong box. Usually, it's made of metal. Always, it has a lock. Strongboxes were invented to keep things like jewels and money safe, so they are super tough. If you lose the key to your strongbox, you're sunk, because it's almost impossible to break one open. If you run it over with a garbage truck,

17

it won't open. If you throw it off the thirty-fifth floor of a building, it won't open (and the people down on the sidewalk will be really mad). If you clobber it with a hammer, it won't open. Okay, maybe if you clobber it with a hammer two hundred times, it might open, but the most important thing about a strongbox is that it's *strong*.

Iggy's grandpa had given him the strongbox for his birthday. At the time, Iggy had been disappointed. "Thanks," he said, because he is an extremely polite person, no matter what other people think.

"It's for keeping things safe," his grandpa explained.

That did not sound very exciting to Iggy. But soon after his birthday, his three-year-old sister, Molly, learned how to draw lips. They were weird-looking lips, big and squooshy, but you could tell they were lips. She drew them with red and pink

markers. At first, she just drew them on drawing paper, but pretty soon, she was drawing them in books, on homework, on clothes, on backpacks, on her stomach, on everything. It was

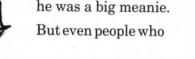

very upsetting, and one of the most upsetting things about it was that Iggy's parents thought it was cute. When Iggy asked them how they'd like to go to school with their homework folder covered in lips, they said, "Oh, Iggy, it's cute!"

(Known fact: These are people who have eaten squid. On purpose.)

So one day, Iggy took Molly's red and pink markers and locked them in his strongbox. This is an event that can be interpreted in several different ways. Some people might say Iggy was creatively and boldly solving a problem. Some people might say he was a big meanie. But even people who

19

said he was a big meanie would have to admit
that once her red and pink markers were gone,
Molly stopped drawing lips and started drawing
waves. Like this:

You could say that by taking her markers,
Iggy helped Molly learn to draw new things.
Really, you could say that.

Anyway, after that, Iggy liked his strongbox.
He especially liked it now, because part one of
his brilliant idea was to lock his good Halloween
candy in his strongbox.

Iggy's strongbox had a top compartment
and a bottom compartment. Iggy moved the
red and pink markers, two used Band-Aids
with dried blood on them (don't worry about
it), and some dead bugs to the bottom com-

partment. Into the top compartment, he put the Skittles, the Kit Kats, the fun-size candy bars, the Reese's peanut butter cups, the Twix, and the peppermint patties and oh yeah, some Starbursts. Then he locked it up and hid the key someplace no one would ever in a million years find it.

Whew. His good candy was safe.

Next, Iggy cleverly brought his strongbox downstairs and placed it next to the window in the family room. This way, any thief who looked in the window, trying to see if there was something he wanted to steal, would catch sight of the strongbox and say to himself, Forget it. These guys have a strongbox. I'd better go on to the next house.

It wasn't as good as an alarm, but it was better than nothing.

Iggy looked at his strongbox and smiled proudly. Part one of his plan was now complete.

But this was only the beginning. The strongbox—even though it was great—was just a backup to parts two and three of Iggy's plan. Because parts two and three would stop

the thief long before he got
anywhere near the window,
the strongbox, or Iggy's
candy.

CHAPTER 4

IGGY IS GENEROUS, KIND, AND HARDWORKING

Did Iggy care only about saving his candy? No! Iggy was generous, kind, and hardworking. He wanted to defend his home and family too.

He knew that if he described or even mentioned the second piece of his plan to his mom or dad, they would say something similar to "You can just forget that." Then their house would be robbed, their computers stolen, and their toaster filled with orange juice. And even though Iggy's good candy would be safe, he (generously) didn't want these bad things to happen to his poor old mom and dad. If their house were robbed, his parents would be sad, they'd be very sad, and even more, they'd be filled with regret because they hadn't listened to him. His mom would put her hands over her face and say "If only we had done what Iggy said." His dad would shake his head. "If only we had listened."

But it would be too late.

So Iggy (kindly) helped his parents avoid regret by not telling them anything about his plan.

Instead he went by himself to the garage and found a shovel. This was not a snow-type shovel. It was a dirt-type shovel. This means that the digging edge was not flat but kind of pointed, like the bottom of a heart. The official name of this kind of shovel is a spade.*

Iggy (hardworkingly) hauled the shovel from the garage to the gate. The gate was on the side of Iggy's house, and it was the line between the front yard path and the back yard path. If you were in the back yard and you opened the

_____

*If you have read the book called *Iggy Is Better Than Ever*, you might be asking, Why are there so many gardening supplies in books about Iggy? And the answer is I don't know. I really don't know.

gate, you would find yourself on a path beside Iggy's house, but if you kept walking, you'd be in the front yard pretty soon, looking at Iggy's front stairs and porch. And if you were in the front yard and you wanted to go into the back yard, you'd follow the path along the side of the house, get to the gate, open it, and ta-da! You'd be in the back yard.

Is this reminding you of something?

Something that happened at the Heckies' house?

If you can't remember, it's in chapter two. Go back and look. I'll wait right here.

　…

　…

　…

Yes! Exactly! The robbers *sneaked through* the gate in order to break in to the Heckies' house.

But that wasn't what was going to happen at Iggy's house, because no robbers were ever going to make it through Iggy's gate.

They might think they were. They might stop in front of Iggy's house, giggle, and say "Yeah, let's go steal all the stuff in this house and wreck their toaster!" Then they'd tiptoe along the path at the side of Iggy's house, thinking that they were going to—giggle, giggle—get to the gate and sneak into his back yard. And then they were going to fall into a massive chasm* and break their legs.

_____

*The word *chasm*, however, has nothing to do with gardening supplies. It means "hole."

CHAPTER 5

IGGY DIGS HIMSELF IN

The path—you know, the one on the side of Iggy's house—was made of big, flat stones. They were heavy, but not so heavy that Iggy couldn't pick them up, especially if he said *"Ahrrr!"* when he did it.

"Ahrrr!"

"Ahrrr!"

"Ahrrr!"

Iggy stopped. He was all sweaty. He reconsidered his plan. Maybe three stones were enough. Did he really need to dig a massive chasm? No.

He just needed to dig a hole deep enough for one thief to fall in and break his leg. One thief screaming "OW OW OW!" would be enough to wake up everyone in the neighborhood. And wasn't that the point?

Yes, it was.

Iggy began to dig. Digging is always the same. First it's easy, then it's hard, and then it's easy again. The beginning is easy because you're fresh and enthusiastic. At least, Iggy was. The dirt flew through the air, the shovel glittered, the pit deepened. After about six and a half minutes, Iggy stopped to admire his

work, and he noticed that the hole he'd dug was not big enough for anyone to fall into. It wasn't deep enough to break anyone's leg.

This was when the easy beginning came to an end and the hard middle began. Iggy didn't feel fresh and enthusiastic anymore. He felt tired and sweaty. But did he give up? No! He (bravely) kept on digging.

And digging.

And digging.

And—

"Whatcha doing?" said a voice right behind him.

"YAAAH!" screeched Iggy in surprise. He whirled around, almost smacking Rudy Heckie with the shovel. "[Thing people sometimes say when they're surprised]!"

Rudy Heckie may have thought he was cool, but Rudy Heckie was only seven. He was kind of skinny and bony too. So when Iggy screeched and almost smacked him with a shovel and said a thing that people sometimes say when they're surprised (but really aren't supposed to say at all), Rudy Heckie was scared. He was so scared he crouched down and put his hands over his face, like he was afraid Iggy was going to hit him. He may have even squeaked in terror.

Iggy felt bad. Staring at Rudy Heckie all curled up in a ball, Iggy remembered that the poor kid's Halloween candy had been stolen, and he was sorry that he had scared the daylights out of him. Not so sorry that he wanted to give him his Skittles or even a single fun-size candy bar, but sorry enough to say, "Sorry, Rudy. You surprised me."

"Mahh," said Rudy. Or maybe it was something else, but Iggy couldn't hear him because Rudy was still rolled up.

"I'm not going to hit you," Iggy said. "I was just surprised." Then he (kindly and generously) added, "You want to help me dig?"

Rudy Heckie peeked through his fingers. "What are you digging?"

Iggy explained that he was digging a thief trap. Iggy (also kindly and generously) didn't explain that he was defending his family, unlike some losers he knew who just let their house get robbed.

"Okay, sure," said Rudy, recovering enough to stand up. "Gimme the shovel."

35

"Okay, but start over here, on this side," Iggy said, handing him the shovel.

"Yeah, whatever," said Rudy, because he was starting to think he was cool again. He began to dig. He wasn't digging exactly where Iggy had told him to dig, but at least he was fresh and enthusiastic. Plus, he dug fast, for such a little bony guy.

For a while, Iggy just watched. The pit was definitely getting wider. It was almost as wide as the path itself now, which was good, because he didn't want the thieves to walk around it. They needed to walk *into* it.

But it wasn't deep enough. "It doesn't need to be any wider," Iggy instructed Rudy. "Make it deeper."

Rudy (rudely) didn't answer. He just kept digging the edges of the pit, making it wider and wider.

"Hey," said Iggy. "Rudy! Make it deeper."

"I am," said Rudy.

He wasn't.

"No you're not!" said Iggy. "Give me back the shovel if you're not going to do it right."

"[Thing no one is supposed to say]!" said Rudy.

Did Iggy rip the shovel out of Rudy's hands and clock him with it? Did Iggy pick Rudy up (which he could have done easily) and throw him into the driveway? Did Iggy grab Rudy by the arm and march him home and tell his parents what Rudy had said?

No. Iggy (kindly and generously) did none of those things.

He merely took the shovel away from Rudy and stepped down into the hole to dig it correctly.

"Give it!" snapped Rudy.

Iggy said a thing that meant "go away." It wasn't the nicest thing in the world, but it wasn't as bad as what Rudy had said.

"No. Gimme the shovel, dude," said Rudy.

Dude? *Dude?* Rudy Heckie was seven. And he was only Iggy's neighbor, not Iggy's friend. There was no way he was allowed to call Iggy dude.

Iggy made a noise. It wasn't the nicest noise in the world, but it wasn't the meanest either. He turned his back to Rudy and kept digging, deeper and deeper. It was hard work. He had to slam the shovel down sharply into the sides of the hole and then scoop the dirt up and out.

But it was worth it. The pit was really starting to get deep.

Yeah.

Then there was a yell and a grunt, and suddenly, Rudy Heckie leapt onto Iggy's back and punched him in the head. "[Bad word]! Got it!" he squalled, grabbing the shovel out of Iggy's hand.

That was stupid.

I mean, think about it: Rudy was holding the shovel with one hand, while he was attached to Iggy's back with the other.

All Iggy had to do was shake him off. Which he did. Rudy crashed to the bottom of the hole. Iggy leaned over, took the shovel back, and started digging again.

Unfortunately, some people don't know when to give up. They have no sense, these people. It's a wonder they've made it this long, these people. Rudy, sadly, was one of these people.

Because what Rudy did then, from his position at the bottom of the pit, was to stick out his hand and try, once more, to grab the shovel away from Iggy.

Just as Iggy was slamming the shovel down as hard as he could.

Oops.

CHAPTER 6

RUDY IS LUCKY

How nice! Rudy Heckie's index finger was not chopped off! How lucky! How great! How fortunate!

But Rudy Heckie had a different interpretation of his finger. Rudy Heckie was not a person who looked at the bright side. Rudy Heckie didn't have a positive attitude. Rudy Heckie saw blood and started to screech, "OW! My finger! My finger!"

"It's still attached," said Iggy, in case Rudy hadn't noticed this good news.

"I'm *bleeding*! *AHHHH!*" He held up his finger. It was definitely bleeding. "You knifed me!"

"I did not. It was a shovel," said Iggy. "And it was your own fault," he added, which wasn't exactly kind or generous, but was his interpretation of the event.

"You slashed me!" Rudy yelled again, waving his bloody hand around so that droplets spattered in the dirt.

"By *mistake*," Iggy explained. "Because you were grabbing the shovel."

"My dad's going to kill you!" Rudy moaned. He was sort of crying.

Don't be a big crybaby, Iggy wanted to say and didn't. Instead, he said the much nicer "It's not even bleeding that much." And then, "I've had a million cuts worse than that." (This, however, was not true.) (See how fair I am?)

Rudy, who was really crying a lot at this point, wrapped his other hand around his bleeding finger and hauled himself out of the pit, which was difficult, because it was pretty deep by now. "You [bad word]!" he said. "[Bad word]! You're gonna be in big trouble." Rudy kicked some dirt into Iggy's hole and went home.

Finally, thought Iggy, and went back to digging.

And digging.

And digging.

Iggy had passed through the hard stretch of digging and reached the second easy bit. This is when you can see that you're close to being done, and suddenly you get enthusiastic again. You think, Wow, I've dug a really deep hole! Only a few more scoops, and I'll be done!

Iggy dug. He was pretty good, in his opinion. Maybe *amazing* was a better word.

He wished his buddies Diego and Arch could see what he'd done. Maybe he'd call them later and invite them over. "Awesome!" they'd say when they saw it.

"Thanks," Iggy would say modestly. "I had to do it. For my family."

"Wow," they'd say. "You are heroic."

Okay, they probably wouldn't *say* that, but they'd be thinking it.

Imagining this scene, Iggy dug and dug until the hole was done.

CHAPTER 7

IGGY IS DESERVING

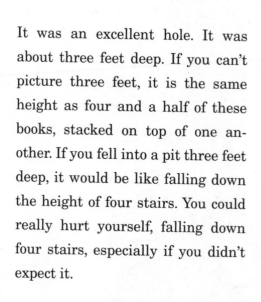

It was an excellent hole. It was about three feet deep. If you can't picture three feet, it is the same height as four and a half of these books, stacked on top of one another. If you fell into a pit three feet deep, it would be like falling down the height of four stairs. You could really hurt yourself, falling down four stairs, especially if you didn't expect it.

Which brings us to the other excellent thing about the hole: It wasn't very wide. It wasn't as wide as it was deep. This meant that it wasn't super noticeable. If you were walking down the path toward the gate and you were busy thinking about the candy and computers you were about to steal, you probably wouldn't notice the hole until you fell into it.

But Iggy wasn't satisfied with "probably." Iggy wanted "certainly." So once Iggy was done digging, he (creatively) dragged the path stones back and laid them on the edges of the hole. Of course, he could only lay them partway over it or else they would have fallen in, but when he got all three of the path stones hanging out over the pit as far as they could go, and shoved another one over a little bit, it looked pretty much like it had before. I mean, it looked like a path. You wouldn't think twice about stepping on it, especially if you were busy thinking about earrings and computers and coins.

Part two was now complete. Iggy

admired his work. But not for very long, because he wasn't done yet. It was now time for part three.

Part three involved Iggy's less-good candy. Remember the less-good candy? The candy that was *not* in his strongbox? This less-good candy had inspired Iggy's brilliant plan. Because what did Iggy know for sure about the thieves who had robbed the Heckies? They liked candy. They had stolen Rudy Heckie's Halloween candy along with the Heckie computers and earrings and coins, which meant that these thieves considered candy right up there with computers.

With this in mind, Iggy had (unselfishly) decided to use his less-good candy to lure the thieves into his trap. In other words, Iggy was going to give his less-good (but certainly not bad) candy away in order to defend his family and their computers and their toaster.

Here is what he did: He took a lollipop and some bubble gum from his bag of less-good candy and put them down on the sidewalk where the driveway began. A few Laffy Taffys midway up the driveway. A lollipop at the top. Two lollipops and some weird round hard candies at the beginning of the path. Bubble gum and weird round hard candies along the path as it ran beside the house. By the time he got to the edge of the thief trap, all he had left were Laffy Taffys, but he had a lot of those. He turned his bag upside down and dumped all of them on the ground.

Iggy stood back and nodded proudly. All three parts of his plan were now complete. He had worked hard and defended his family. He deserved a rest. And a snack. And a trophy.

Stepping carefully around the hole, Iggy went through the gate to his back yard and into his house.

CHAPTER 8

NOBODY APPRECIATES IGGY

Have you ever been proud or excited about something you've done, tried to tell someone about it, and been ignored or, worse yet, insulted?

Yeah. I thought so.

Basically, that is the definition of being a kid.

But usually, the people ignoring or insulting you are grown-ups. Iggy, who was feeling proud and excited about his trap, didn't even want to tell any grown-ups about it. He knew what the grown-ups would say. But when he went inside, he found Maribel and Molly together in the family room, with no grown-ups around.

"Hey, you guys!" said Iggy excitedly. "Guess what I just did! I just dug this most awesome—"

"Shh," said Maribel, not looking up from her book. "I'm reading."

Iggy scowled. "Fine," he said, "go ahead and read. But if it weren't for me, you could probably say good-bye to all your candy tonight—"

"*Shh!*" hissed Maribel, still not looking up from her book. "Nobody cares."

"Lookit," said Molly. She had drawn a wave on her stomach. "Tsunami!" She shook her stomach.

"Try drawing a crime wave," Iggy said. "Be-

cause that's what we'd be in if it weren't for—"

"Be *quiet*," said Maribel. "For once in your life."

"Whoosh, whoosh," said Molly. She was still shaking her stomach. "Oh no! There's a boat!" She drew a little boat on her stomach.

"Mom!" yelled Maribel. "These guys won't leave me alone!"

"Kids! Let Maribel read!" said Iggy's mom, appearing in the doorway.

"Why do *we* have to be quiet?" asked Iggy (reasonably). "Isn't this the family room? Aren't we the family?"

"Well—" began Mom.

"Mom!" moaned Maribel. "I'm in a *really* exciting part. Make them go away."

"All right, all right," said Mom. "Molly, sweetie, you come and help me start dinner. Iggy, go find someplace else to be."

"This is totally unfair!" Iggy roared. He kicked a table leg. "Has Maribel been outside fighting crime all day? No! Why is she the boss of this house when I'm the one protecting it!"

Iggy's mom sighed. "I have no idea what you're talking about, Iggy. But you need to go to your room and cool down."

"Time-out for Iggy," said Molly. She waved. "Bye, Iggy."

They should be showering him with thanks. They should be carrying him around on their

shoulders. They should be giving him a trophy.

Instead, they were sending him to his room.

His family did not deserve him.

Iggy stomped upstairs.

CHAPTER 9

IT'S NICE AND COZY IN THE CLOSET

In his room, Iggy did some more stomping. Also some muttering. He thumped his pillow. He kicked his shoe across the room. He was going to run away. He was going to run away to Ketchum, Idaho. Yeah, he was! He put some socks into his backpack. Yeah! A sweatshirt.

Yeah! Some money. A flashlight. Yeah! They'd be sorry. This would teach them. "How could we have been so wrong!" they'd groan when they discovered the thief trap he'd made with his own hands. "Our only son, exhausting himself to defend us! And we never even thanked him! We didn't deserve such a son!"

Then they'd cry, especially his mom. They'd feel bad. They'd feel rotten.

It made Iggy sad, thinking about how rotten his mom was going to feel.

His family didn't understand him. They didn't appreciate him. They thought they did, but they didn't.

It was hard, being so misunderstood.

Iggy lay down on his old, hairy rug to think about how misunderstood he was. It was

comfortable, his old, hairy rug. He yawned. Maybe he didn't need to leave *this minute*. It was going to get dark soon. He didn't really need to run away in the *dark*. He thought about the candy in his strongbox. Maybe he didn't need to run away at all. They were his family, after all. He'd give them a second chance, even Maribel.

Because that's the kind of person he was: generous, kind, unselfish . . .

Lying there on his old, hairy rug, Iggy pictured a thief crashing down into his pit, and his mom and dad and Maribel rushing outside to discover what he'd done for them. He would smile patiently. "It's okay," he would say as they apologized.

Iggy heard the doorbell ring. The front door was underneath his room.

He practiced smiling patiently.

"I've got it!" called his mom's voice, coming down the hall below.

Iggy kept smiling patiently.

"Carl!" said Iggy's mom. "Hi!"

Iggy froze.

"Laurel!" Mr. Heckie boomed. "Would you like to know where I spent the last four hours?"

Iggy got up and opened the door to his room.

"Um—" said Iggy's mom. She sounded like she didn't want to know where Mr. Heckie had spent the last four hours.

Mr. Heckie told her anyway. "I'll tell you, Laurel! At the *emergency room*! Because your son almost cut off Rudy's finger!"

"Iggy?" said Mom, like she might have another son.

Very quietly, Iggy stepped out into the upstairs hall.

"Tell her, Rudy. Tell her what Iggy did!" ordered Mr. Heckie.

"Iggy slashed me with a giant shovel!" squeaked Rudy. His voice was very high compared to Mr. Heckie's. "And look what happened!" There was a pause while Rudy probably held up his bloody finger.

"Five stitches, Laurel!"

Iggy began to edge along the wall.

"Yeah!" said Rudy. "Five!"

"Iggy did that?" said his mom again. "But he doesn't have a giant shovel."

"Yes he does!" Rudy cried. "He dug a huge hole with it, and then he pushed me in and slashed me with it!"

(Is this an example of an event being open to interpretation, or is this a plain old lie? I will let you answer that for yourself. But I will also point out that Rudy's description of this event does not include any of his own actions. The little weasel.)

"Iggy!" called Iggy's mom.

Iggy dove into the hall closet.

"Iggy! Come down here!"

It was nice and cozy in there, with the coats and jackets.

"I'll get him!" said Maribel, thumping up the stairs. What a busybody. "He's not in here!" she called from his room.

Iggy decided to stay in the hall closet forever.

"Iggy!" hollered Molly.

"Iggy!" hollered his dad.

The only problem with the closet was that Iggy could hear everything they said. He wished he couldn't.

"I'm so sorry about your finger, Rudy," said Iggy's mom. "I will definitely talk to Iggy and find out what happened."

"Oh, we know what happened, Laurel!" growled Mr. Heckie. "Your Iggy hit my Rudy with a shovel!"

"But what was he doing with this shovel?" asked Iggy's mom. She sounded very confused. "And why would he hit Rudy with it?"

"He was digging a trap," said Rudy truthfully.

"A trap?" asked Iggy's mom. "What kind of trap?"

"I'll show you!" offered Rudy. "Come on!"

CHAPTER 10

IGGY SEES THE FUTURE

Do you know what the word *self-sacrificing* means? Don't worry! I'm about to tell you. Self-sacrificing is like unselfishness-plus. It's like unselfishness with whipped cream on top. When you are unselfish, you think about other people before yourself. When you are self-sacrificing, you actually allow bad things to happen to you so that they don't happen to other people.

It isn't easy, being self-sacrificing.

If someone tells you it's easy, they're lying.

Take Iggy, for example. It would have been easy for Iggy to stay in the hall closet for the next few hours. Then, after Mr. Heckie and

Rudy were gone and after his parents had calmed down, Iggy could come out and explain his side of the story. His parents might not be *happy* with him at that point, but they wouldn't be as mad as they were in this instant. By then, they might even be able to understand that he'd dug the trap to protect them. They might even—long shot, but still—think he was bold and creative.

Another thing that would have been easy: running away to Ketchum, Idaho. His backpack was all packed and ready to go.

But—

But—

As Iggy stood there in the closet, he looked into the future, not the distant future, but the next four and a half minutes of the future. And he saw what the future held: squeaky, bony Rudy Heckie leading his mom toward disaster. Why? Because Rudy was rushing along the path with Iggy's mom behind him. Rudy knew exactly where Iggy's trap was, so Rudy was going stop before he fell into it. But Iggy's mom didn't know a thing. And it was getting dark too. She wouldn't see that the path was changed. She'd fall right into it. And then she'd break her leg.

It was Iggy and Iggy alone who could stop this from happening.

Iggy was standing between his mom and a broken leg.

So what did Iggy do? Did he do the easy thing and stay in the closet? Did he run into his room, grab his backpack, and disappear forever?

No, he did not.

Iggy bravely, generously, and, above all, self-sacrificingly tore out of the closet, down the stairs, out the front door, and around the side of the house, screaming.

OOOOOOOOOOO

CHAPTER 11

THE PIT
AND THE PRIMATE

Iggy screamed, rounding the corner of his house.

Then three things happened, one right after the other:

1. Iggy's mom stopped and whirled around. "About time you showed up, young man!" she said.
2. Rudy Heckie noticed Iggy's Laffy Taffy on the path. "Hey! Candy!" he said, and bent down to pick it up.

3. Mr. Heckie, looking over his shoulder to see what all the screaming was about, tripped over Rudy, crashed through the paving stones, and landed with a not-very-good sound right smack in the middle of Iggy's trap.

• • •

You know that humans (us) are animals, right? It's not too surprising. Obviously, we aren't rocks or vegetables. We aren't funguses either, even though some people act like they are. We are part of the animal kingdom. We are a specific part: We are primates. That means that we have a lot in common with cute little monkeys and some weird little guys called lorises.* Among the things we have in common with cute little monkeys and weird little lorises and every other primate is a tail.

No, really!

We *do* have tails, but only for a week or two before we're born. Our bodies kind of grow around them, so by the time we're born, we don't have them anymore. Which is really too bad. Anyway, the point is this: Inside you, at the bottom of your spine, right near your tush, there are a few little bones that are what's left of your tail. Many people even call this a tailbone. There's another word for it, but it's too hard to spell, so I'll call it a tailbone too.

_____

*If you look them up, be sure to check out their fingers!

77

This is the part of Mr. Heckie that made the not-very-good sound when he landed in Iggy's trap.

Directly after that, Mr. Heckie made a not-very-good sound too.

Because he was a primate and he had broken his tail.

Ouch.

Poor Mr. Heckie. He thought he had already spent too much time in the emergency room that day, when really, he had hours and hours more to go. In fact, Mr. Heckie spent *all* the rest of that day and a little bit of the next one in the emergency room. Poor Mr. Heckie.

"What happened to Mr. Heckie in the emergency room?" you ask, because you are a caring person. "Did he get a cast?"

Nope. You can't put a cast on a tailbone.

NOPE,

"Did he get stitches?"

Nope. There wasn't anything to stitch.

"Did he get surgery?"

Nope.

"Did he get a shot with a big needle?"

Nope.

"Did he get horrible-tasting medicine?"

Nope.

"What the heck *did* happen to Mr. Heckie?" you ask.

The doctor gave him a special cushion to sit on. And some aspirin.

Yes. That's all.

Do you remember back in chapter six when Rudy Heckie's finger was not chopped off? Do you remember how Rudy Heckie refused to look on the bright side? How he had a negative attitude and thought only about his problems and not about how they could have been much worse?

Well, guess what! Rudy Heckie had inherited this negative attitude from his dad. Mr. Heckie didn't look at the bright side either. He did *not* say to himself, Wow, I'm lucky! At least I didn't have to get stitches or surgery or a shot with a big needle or horrible-tasting medicine!

He said, "What a disaster! I broke my tail-bone!" And right after that, he said, "And it's all Iggy Frangi's fault!"

CHAPTER 12

MR. HECKIE'S TAILBONE, INTERPRETED

I'm sure you will not be surprised to learn that there were several different interpretations of this event.

Actually, there were only two. Here's the first interpretation:

1.
Iggy is bad.

Several people had this interpretation. Among them was Mr. Heckie. He said, "Iggy dug the hole I fell into. So it's his fault I have a broken tailbone. I hope that kid gets the punishment he deserves!"

Rudy Heckie was also in this group. He said, "First, Iggy threw me into his hole; then he slashed me with a giant shovel! On purpose! I had to get five stitches! Then he broke my dad's butt!"

Even Maribel, Iggy's own sister, said, "I can't believe what a moron you are. Danita Heckie is never going to speak to me again."

But there was a second interpretation! A better, *wiser* interpretation that took into account the many complex small events that led to the large event of Mr. Heckie breaking his tailbone.

2.
Iggy is a hero.

Unfortunately, there was only one person who had this interpretation, and that was Iggy. But, hoping to help his parents to arrive at this interpretation too, he said, "Okay, yeah, it's true that I dug the hole, but Mr. Heckie fell into it all by himself. It's not like I pushed him. He fell over his own kid. His own kid, who was about to eat candy off the ground, which you're always telling me not to do. Because Rudy's a pig, his dad tripped over him, so if it's anyone's fault Mr. Heckie broke his you-know-what, it's Rudy's. And no way did I throw Rudy Heckie into that hole! He's such a liar! The little jerk jumped me and tried to grab the shovel away from me. *That's* how he got hurt. *I* didn't do it. I mean, I *did* it, but not on purpose. I was just digging, and he got in the way. He also hit me on the head, in case you're interested. And—in case you're interested—I was digging that pit to protect you guys: *your* earrings, *your* computers, and *your* toaster. And I worked hard too; I worked really hard for a really long time, all by myself. Rudy was only there for, like, three minutes, and he *wanted* to be there. And—in case you haven't noticed—I made a really good trap. If a thief had fallen into it and broken *his* tailbone, you'd be *happy*. You'd say 'Wow, thanks, Iggy! What a great thing you did!' And also—in case you haven't noticed—I saved *you* too, Mom. I ran downstairs to keep *you* from breaking your leg, even when I knew I was going to get in trouble.

Some moms might say 'Thank you for saving me from breaking my leg. What a great son you are!' Some parents would be *happy* I did that. Some parents would be happy I didn't run away. Which I could have. Some parents would be saying 'How can we thank you enough for all your work?' They would!"

Iggy stopped, but only because he had run out of breath. When he got some more, he added, "I don't think I should have any punishment at all. I think I should get a reward."

Iggy's mom and dad looked at each other. Then Iggy's mom said, "We'll be back in a minute." Then they got up and went into the computer room and closed the door.

"They're deciding what to do to you," said Maribel. "I hope they lock you in the basement. Moron."

"I hope they lock *you* in the basement," said Iggy. But he didn't really mean it. What was the use? Maribel never did anything wrong. Why was that? "Go stand outside the door and listen," he said to Molly. "And then come tell me what they're saying." Molly was only three. She never got in trouble for anything. Why was he the only one?

Molly came back. "Rrruh," she said.

Rrruh? Iggy frowned at Molly. Rrruh could be anything. Nothing is more open to interpretation than rrruh. Rrruh could be rah, as in Rah! Iggy is a hero! It probably wasn't that kind of rrruh. It was probably a bad rrruh, like Rrruh, I've had enough of this kid. Can you think of anyplace we could send him? Rrruh could even be the worst thing: a crying rrruh. Was his mom crying?

Iggy really hoped not. Maybe his mom was crying because they had decided to get rid of him and she felt bad about it.

Iggy felt bad about it too.

He heard the door to the computer room open. He heard his mom and dad walk down the hall.

Iggy covered his face with a sofa pillow.

"Iggy . . ." his mom began.

CHAPTER 13

BLAAAAAAAAAAHHHHHHHHHHHH

Here is Iggy's interpretation of what his parents said:

"Your father and I are very disappointed in you. We expect more blaaaaaaaaahhhhhhhhhhh and blaaaaaaaaahhhhhhhhhhh from someone your age, and we would hope that you blaaa-aaaaaahhhhhhhhhhhh. But instead, you blaaa-aaaaaahhhhhhhhhhhh. [*They're mad,* Iggy thought.] As far as blaaaaaaaaahhhhhhhhhhh, you know blaaaaaaaaahhhhhhhhhhh and blaaaaaaaaahhhhhhhhhhh. [*I'm in big trouble.*]

You simply cannot blaaaaaahhhhh-hhhhhhhh. You know better than that! Blaaaaaaaaahhhhhhhhhhhhh. But [*A "but"! Yay!*] we don't consider what happened to Mr. Heckie to be your responsibility [*Good, because it isn't!*] and blaaaaaaaaahhhhhhhhhhhhh and blaaaaaaaaahhhhhhhhhhhhh. However [*Uh-oh.*], tomorrow, you will be responsible for refilling that hole with dirt and putting the stones back where you found them [*That's it? That's all? SWEET! Yes! Iggy is the MAN!*] and—are you paying attention, Iggy?"

"Yes!" said Iggy. His mom and dad were so cool! He loved them!

"Since you *did* cut Rudy's finger—we believe that it was an accident, but you *did* cut his finger—and since poor Rudy lost all his Halloween candy in the robbery [*They are not, they* wouldn't.], you will give your candy to him [*NOOOOOOOOOOO!*]."

"NOOOOOOOOOOO!" moaned Iggy.

"Yes," said his mom. "Along with an apology."

"Yes," said his dad. "And you'll do it now."

CHAPTER 14

IGGY DIGS HIMSELF OUT

Sadly, Iggy pulled the three stones of the path out of the pit, where they had fallen when Mr. Heckie crashed onto them. Once the stones were out of the way, he stared at the hole. It was big. It was going to take a lot of work to fill it up again. He was only a kid. He was too young to have to do all this work by himself.

He went inside and said this to his dad.

His dad was stretched out on the couch, watching the Lakers pound the Cavs.

Guess what his dad said.

Right. He said, "You dug it. You can fill it up again."

"I'm only a kid," said Iggy. "I'm not the Incredible Hulk."

"Think about Rudy eating your candy bars," said his dad. "You'll be just like the Hulk in no time."

Iggy went back to his hole and began shoveling dirt while thinking about his Twix, his Skittles, his fun-size candy bars, his Reese's peanut butter cups, and his peppermint patties.

For some reason, the peppermint patties made him the maddest. Rudy Heckie probably didn't even like peppermint patties. He had probably thrown them away, right after he'd taken the candy, said "Okay, thanks," and closed the door on Iggy, who had then slumped away, holding a strongbox that contained only used Band-Aids, red and pink markers, and dead bugs.

Surprise! Iggy was almost finished filling the

hole with dirt. Wow. Dad was right. Time flies when you're enraged. After a few more minutes, which Iggy spent thinking about Rudy Heckie eating his Skittles, he was done. All the dirt that he had taken out of the ground the day before was back in it. He jumped up and down on the dirt a few times to make it flat.

Then he dragged the path stones back into place.

"*Ahrrr!*"

"*Ahrrr!*"

"*Ahrrr!*"

It was a path again. Iggy sighed. It had been a good trap. He had made it himself, and now it was all gone. Except—

Iggy picked up one of the weird round hard candies he had put on the ground to lure the thieves into his trap. There was a tiny bit of dirt on the wrapper, that's all. He wiped it on his pants. It was still candy. And it was all the candy he was going to get for a while.

He found another one. And then a Laffy Taffy. And a lollipop.

Iggy collected his not-very-good-but-now-only candy and put it in the top compartment of his strongbox. Since he didn't consider bubble gum to be candy at all, he unwrapped a piece and put it in his mouth. It was so hard he almost couldn't chew it, but at least it was sweet. After lunch, he would eat a lollipop, he decided. And after dinner, maybe a Laffy Taffy. It was better than nothing.

But not *much* better.

He sighed and put the strongbox back where it had been when it had had good candy in it, next to the family room window.

"You all done?" asked his dad from the couch.

"Yeah."

"I'm sorry about your candy, kid," his dad said. He slapped the pillow next to him. "Come watch the game. Fourth quarter, Lakers up, ninety-eight to eighty-seven."

CHAPTER 15

ONE WEEK LATER

It was actually only five days later, but "One Week Later" is a better chapter title.

Five days later, it was a Friday night, and Iggy's family went out for dinner. They went to their favorite restaurant, which was called El Segundo, which means "The Second," even though there was no restaurant called El Primero, which means "The First." Oh well. It was still Iggy's family's favorite restaurant. Iggy had a burrito with extra guacamole. He always had that.

After he had gobbled it down, he and Maribel and (sort of) Molly played mini golf out in the back yard of the restaurant while his parents talked about whatever parents spend so much time talking about.

Everyone in Iggy's family always had a great time at El Segundo.

Eventually, Iggy's parents were done talking about that thing parents talk about. They came out to the mini-golf course and said it was time to go. Iggy suggested that they stop for ice cream on the way home.

What a fantastic suggestion! said his parents. Sure! Let's all go get hot fudge sundaes!

AHAHA! Of course they didn't say that!

They said No.

So Iggy and his family drove home, and everything was just the way it always was until they pulled into their driveway.

After they had pulled into their driveway, but before they had opened the car doors to get out, Iggy's dad said, "Hey, who left the gate open?"

Nobody had time to answer before two guys in dark clothes came rushing past the car and down the driveway to the street.

"Everyone stay where you are!" said Iggy's mom, which was a very intelligent thing to say.

So they sat in the car while Iggy's dad called the police.

After Officer Collops (I can't help it. That was her name.) and Officer Lai inspected Iggy's house and determined that there were no more thieves in it, the Frangi family went inside.

They came in nervously, afraid of what they might see. Were their computers missing? Was Iggy's mom's jewelry gone? Was the toaster filled with orange juice? Had Maribel's jar of coins been taken? Even Molly was worried—about her stuffie, Claire Plum. What if she'd been kidnapped?

They tiptoed around, feeling strange, even though it was their own house.

Iggy's dad came out of the computer room. "Computers are all here."

Iggy's mom came downstairs. "All my jewelry's okay."

Maribel said, "My jar is right where I left it."

Molly said, "Claire Plum is scared." But she was holding her when she said it.

Iggy's dad even looked in the toaster. No orange juice.

"My strongbox is gone!" yelled Iggy, rushing into the room.

Officer Collops and Officer Lai were very sympathetic. "I'm sorry about that," said Officer Lai. She got out a special pad of paper. "Tell me the contents, and I'll put it in the report. Sometimes we recover stolen goods. You never know—you might get your things back."

Iggy frowned, trying to remember exactly. "Okay," he said slowly. "I think I was down to three banana Laffy Taffys. One grape lollipop. Two bubble gums, but it's okay if you don't find those. And, hm, not sure—maybe *six* of those weird round hard candies? You know, the ones that hurt the top of your mouth. I don't know what they're called. Plus four markers, some dead bugs, which I need, and two Band-Aids with blood on them."

Officer Lai put down her special pad. "Where was this strongbox?" she asked.

Iggy told her about putting it in the window to show thieves that they should skip his house and rob the neighbors.

When he was done, there was a moment of silence. Then Officer Collops said, "They probably broke in *because* they saw a strongbox in the window."

Both Iggy's mom and Iggy's dad looked at him with squinty eyes.

"They probably thought they were going to get some cash," said Officer Lai. "Or valuables."

"They probably still think it," said Officer Collops. She made a snorty sound.

Then Iggy's mom made a snorty sound too. "It was a real strongbox, not a toy."

"It's going to take a lot of work to get it open," said Iggy's dad. Iggy didn't understand why he was smiling.

"And probably a sledgehammer," said Iggy's mom.

"Or a crowbar," said Officer Lai. "Sometimes that'll do it."

"Or a metal drill," said Officer Collops.

"I hope they have to buy a metal drill," said Iggy's mom.

"I hope it costs them a lot of money," said Iggy's dad.

Suddenly, Officer Collops and Officer Lai started laughing. So did Iggy's mom and dad. "I hope it takes them hours to get it open," said Iggy's dad.

"And once they do get it open," gasped Iggy's mom, "I hope they like the Band-Aids."

"I hope they like banana Laffy Taffy," gasped Officer Lai.

She was laughing so hard she was almost choking.

"Hey!" said Iggy. "That was *my* banana Laffy Taffy."

Iggy's dad was laughing so much that Iggy could barely understand him when he said, "Son, tomorrow I'll buy you as much Laffy Taffy as you can eat."

Iggy thought fast. "How about four peppermint patties, a Reese's, and a regular-size Twix instead?" he suggested.

"Deal!" said Iggy's dad, when he could talk.

For some minutes, Iggy sat there, watching the grown-ups laugh. What was so funny? Their house had been robbed. *He* had been robbed.

If they had let him leave the thief trap where it was, the thief would be lying in it right now, yelling "OW OW OW!"

Wouldn't that be better?

Iggy looked around the room at all the laughing grown-ups. They were happy. And he was

107

happy, because he was going to get some good candy the next day. Molly's pink and red markers were gone forever, which was also good. The robbers were probably going to be disappointed when they finally got the strongbox open, unless they really loved banana Laffy Taffy, which Iggy doubted. Maybe they would even decide to give

up robbing houses out of disappointment. Maybe, thought Iggy, he *had* stopped a crime wave.

After all, none of these things would have happened without him.

If it weren't for him, the grown-ups would be their regular not-laughing selves, the robbers would be planning their next crime, Molly would

learn how to draw hearts, and he would have no candy left.

Yeah, thought Iggy, I am pretty much the hero of this story.

That was his interpretation, anyway.

Many things are open to interpretation in this world, but not **ANNIE BARROWS**. *Fact:* She has never done one bad thing in her entire life. Pushing her sister off the boat dock? A mistake! A mistake that could happen to anyone! Writing on the wall with lipstick? Decoration! The thing with the cat? Nonsense! The cat had a great time.

anniebarrows.com
@anniebarrowsauthor

SAM RICKS has ample experience digging physical and metaphorical holes. Since 1987, he is the proud owner of a strongbox. Never far from purple or pink markers, he spends his days drawing lips, waves, and miscellany. As of this publication, he has never been to Ketchum, Idaho.

samricks.com
@samuelricks

DON'T MISS IGGY'S NEXT TRIUMPHS

COMING SOON!